To my grandmother GG—
I hope I inherited a fraction of your
strength, wit, intellect, and grit! You amaze me.
Happy birthday!
—K. W.

For party planners everywhere
—J. C.

THE BEAR BOOKS
MARGARET K. McELDERRY BOOKS
An imprint of Simon & Schuster Children's Publishing Division
1230 Avenue of the Americas, New York, New York 10020
Text copyright © 2021 by Karma Wilson
Illustrations copyright © 2021 by Jane Chapman
All rights reserved, including the right of reproduction in whole or in part in any form.
MARGARET K. MCELDERRY BOOKS is a trademark of Simon & Schuster, Inc.
For information about special discounts for bulk purchases, please contact Simon & Schuster Special Sales at 1-866-506-1949 or business@simonandschuster.com.
The Simon & Schuster Speakers Bureau can bring authors to your live event. For more information or to book an event,
contact the Simon & Schuster Speakers Bureau at 1-866-248-3049 or visit our website at www.simonspeakers.com.
Book design by Lauren Rille
The text for this book was set in Adobe Caslon.
The illustrations for this book were rendered in acrylic paint.
Manufactured in China
0121 SCP
First Edition
2 4 6 8 10 9 7 5 3 1
Library of Congress Cataloging-in-Publication Data
Names: Wilson, Karma, author. | Chapman, Jane, illustrator.
Title: Bear can't wait / by Karma Wilson ; illustrated by Jane Chapman.
Other titles: Bear cannot wait
Description: First edition. | New York : Margaret K. McElderry Books, 2021. | Series: The Bear books ; [10] | Audience: Ages 4-8. | Audience: Grades K-1. |
Summary: As final preparations are being made for a long-planned surprise party, Bear gets so excited he nearly ruins everything.
Identifiers: LCCN 2019025841 (print) | LCCN 2019025842 (ebook) | ISBN 9781481459754 (hardcover) | ISBN 9781481459761 (ebook)
Subjects: CYAC: Stories in rhyme. | Patience—Fiction. | Parties—Fiction. | Surprise—Fiction. | Bears—Fiction. | Forest animals—Fiction.
Classification: LCC PZ8.3.W6976 Bao 2021 (print) | LCC PZ8.3.W6976 (ebook) | DDC [E]—dc23
LC record available at https://lccn.loc.gov/2019025841
LC ebook record available at https://lccn.loc.gov/2019025842

Bear Can't Wait

Karma Wilson

illustrations by Jane Chapman

MARGARET K. McELDERRY BOOKS
New York London Toronto Sydney New Delhi

On a bright, sunny day,
Bear paces to and fro.
He fusses and he fidgets.
"Why is time so slow?"

"For so many weeks
I have planned a surprise.

"But it's not till tonight,"
Bear says with a sigh.

He looks toward the sun,
but the day's just begun.

But the bear
can't
wait!

Gopher, Mouse, and Mole
all stroll down the trail
with goodies packed up
in an old tin pail.

Mouse squeaks, "Stoke the fire.
Get ready to bake.
Gopher's dug carrots
for sweet carrot cake!"

Gathered in the den,
they cook for a friend.

But the bear
can't
wait!

Badger stops by
to help them get ready,
with a basket full of berries
and a sack of confetti.

Raven brings a candle
and Owl brings flowers.
Bear asks, "Is it time?"
But there's still TWO hours!

Bear frets and he fiddles.
He wiggles and he twiddles,

since the **bear**
can't
wait!

"Chip chop! Get to work!"
Mole says with a clap.
"There's cake to be frosted
and presents to wrap!"

Bear raises his paw.
"Let me do the cake!"
He rushes in to help,
when he trips by mistake . . .

BOOM,
BANG!
SPLAT!

The cake is squished flat . . .

because Bear

couldn't

wait!

Bear sees his mess,
and with tears in his eyes
he says, "Now I've done it.
I've wrecked our surprise."

Mouse squeaks, "Maybe not!
We still have an hour.
Go! Get more carrots
and honey and flour!

"There's much to be done.
Hurry, Bear, RUN!"

And the bear
doesn't
wait!

Time is almost up,
but Bear is very fast.
They bake a new cake
even better than the last!

They hustle and they bustle
while they decorate the den,
and just when they're finished . . .

they all hear Wren.
"Hurry and hide!
He's almost inside!"

And the bear
can't
wait!

Underneath his quilt,
Bear hides with a grin.
He tries not to giggle
when Hare hops in!

They all shout, "Surprise!
Happy birthday, Hare!"
"We planned you a party
as a gift," says Bear.

"There's presents and cake,
so let's celebrate!"

And the hare
can't
wait!